PUFFIN BOOKS

Published by the Penguin Group
Penguin Books Ltd, 80 Strand, London WC2R 0RL, England
Penguin Group (USA), Inc., 375 Hudson Street, New York, New York 10014, USA
Penguin Books Australia Ltd, 250 Camberwell Road, Camberwell, Victoria 3124, Australia
Penguin Books Canada Ltd, 10 Alcorn Avenue, Toronto, Ontario, Canada M4V 3B2
Penguin Books India (P) Ltd, 11 Community Centre, Panchsheel Park, New Delhi – 110 017, India
Penguin Group (NZ), cnr Airborne and Rosedale Roads, Albany, Auckland 1310, New Zealand
Penguin Books (South Africa) (Pty) Ltd, 24 Sturdee Avenue, Rosebank 2196, South Africa

Penguin Books Ltd, Registered Offices: 80 Strand, London WC2R 0RL, England

www.penguin.com

First published by J. M. Dent & Sons Ltd 1985
Published in Picture Puffins 1987
Reissued in Puffin Books 1995
25 24 23 22 21

Text copyright © Margaret Mahy, 1972, 1985
Illustrations copyright © Margaret Chamberlain, 1985
All rights reserved

Library of Congress Catalog card number: 87–50337

Made and printed in Italy by Printer Trento Srl

British Library Cataloguing in Publication Data
A CIP catalogue record for this book is available from the British Library

ISBN-13: 978-0-14055-430-4

The Man Whose Mother Was a Pirate

Margaret Mahy

Illustrated by Margaret Chamberlain

PUFFIN BOOKS

There was once a little man who had never seen the sea, although his mother was an old pirate woman. The two of them lived in a great city far, far from the seashore.

The little man always wore a respectable brown suit and respectable brown shoes. He worked in a neat office, and wrote down rows of figures in books, ruling lines under them.

Well, one day his mother said, "Shipmate, I want to
see the sea again. I want to fire my old silver pistol, and
see the waves jump with surprise."

"Oh, Mother!" said the little man. "We haven't got a car, or a bicycle, or a horse. And we've no money, either. All we have is a wheelbarrow and a kite."

"We must make do!" his mother answered sharply. "I will go and load my pistol and polish my cutlass."

The little man went to work.

"Please, Mr Fat," he begged his boss, "please may I have two weeks' holiday to take my mother to the seaside?"

"I don't go to the seaside!" said Mr Fat crossly. "Why should you?"

"It is for my mother," the little man explained. "She used to be a pirate."

"Oh, well, that's different," said Mr Fat who rather wished he were a pirate himself. "But make sure you are back in two weeks, or I will buy a computer."

So off they set, the little man pushing his mother in the wheelbarrow, and his mother holding the kite. His mother wore a green scarf and gold earrings. Between her lips was her old black pipe, behind one ear a crimson rose. The little man wore his brown suit buttoned, and his brown shoes tied. He trotted along pushing the wheelbarrow.

As they went, his mother talked about the sea. She told him of its voices.

"It sings with a booming voice and smiles as it slaps
the ships. It screams or sadly sighs. There are many
voices in the sea and a lot of gossip, too. Where are the
great whales sailing? Is the ice moving in Hudson Bay?
What is the weather in Tierra del Fuego? The sea
knows the answers to a lot of questions, and one wave
tells another."

"Oh yes, Mother," said the little man whose shoes
hurt him rather.

"Where are you off to?" asked a farmer.

"I'm taking my mother to the seaside," said the little man.

"I wouldn't go there myself," said the farmer. "It's up and down with the waves, in and out with the tide. The sea doesn't stay put the way a good hill does."

"My mother likes things that don't stay put," said the little man.

Something began to sing in the back of his mind. "Could that be the song of the sea?" he wondered, as he pushed the wheelbarrow. His mother rested her chin on her knees.

"Yes, it's blue in the sunshine," she said, "and it's grey in the rain. I've seen it golden with sunlight, silver with moonlight and black as ink at night. It's never the same twice."

They came to a river. There was no boat. The little man tied the wheelbarrow to the kite. A wind blew by, ruffling his collar, teasing his neat moustache.

"Hold tight, Mother!" he called.

Up in the air they went as the wind took the kite. The little man dangled from the kite string. His mother swung in her wheelbarrow-basket.

"This is all very well, Sam," she shouted to him. "But the sea – ah, the sea! It tosses you up and pulls you down. It speeds you along, it holds you still. It storms you and calms you. There's a bit of everything in the sea."

"Yes, Mother," the little man said. The singing in the back of his mind was growing louder and louder. As he dangled from the kite string the white wings of the birds in the sky began to look like the white wings of ships at sea.

The kite let them down gently on the other side of the river.

"Where are you going?" asked a philosopher fellow who sat reading under a tree.

"I'm taking my mother to the sea," said the little man.

"What misery!" cried the philosopher.

"Well, I didn't much like the idea to start with," said the little man, "but now there's this song in the back of my mind. I'm beginning to think I might like the sea when I get there."

"Go back, go back, little man," cried the philosopher.

"The wonderful things are never as wonderful as you
hope they'll be. The sea is less warm, the joke less
funny, the taste is never as good as the smell."

"Hurry up! The sea is calling," shouted the pirate
mother, waving her cutlass from the wheelbarrow.

The little man trundled his mother away, and as he ran he noticed that his brown suit had lost all its buttons.

Then something new came into the wind's scent.
"Glory! Glory! There's the salt!" cried his mother triumphantly.

Suddenly they came over the hill.

Suddenly there was the sea.

The little man could only stare. He hadn't dreamed of the BIGNESS of the sea. He hadn't dreamed of the blueness of it. He hadn't thought it would roll like kettledrums, and swish itself on to the beach. He opened his mouth, and the drift and the dream of it, the weave and the wave of it, the fume and foam of it never left him again. At his feet the sea stroked the sand with soft little paws. Farther out, the great, graceful breakers moved like kings into court, trailing the peacock-patterned sea behind them.

The little man and his pirate mother danced
hippy-hoppy-happy hornpipes up and down the beach.
The little man's clothes blew about in the wind,
delighted to be free at last.

A rosy sea captain stopped to watch them.

"Well, here are two likely people," he cried. "Will you be my bo'sun, Madam? And you, little man, you can be my cabin boy."

"Thank you!" said the little man.

"Say, 'Aye, aye, sir!'" roared the captain.

"Aye, aye, sir!" replied the little man just as smartly as if he'd been saying, 'Aye, aye, sir!' all his life.

So Sailor Sam went on board with his pirate mother and the sea captain, and a year later someone brought Mr Fat a green glass bottle with a letter in it.

"Having a wonderful time," the letter read. "Why don't you run off to sea, too?"

And if you want any more moral to the story than this, you must go to sea and find it.